Dandy the Lion

Helping Others

written and illustrated by:

Kasey Shaver

Archway Publishing books may be ordered
through booksellers or by contacting:

Archway Publishing
1663 Liberty Drive
Bloomington, IN 47403
www.archwaypublishing.com
1 (888) 242-5904

This is a work of fiction. All of the characters,
names, incidents, organizations, and dialogue
in this novel are either the products of the
author's imagination or are used fictitiously.

Because of the dynamic nature of the Internet, any
web addresses or links contained in this book may
have changed since publication and may no longer
be valid. The views expressed in this work are
solely those of the author and do not necessarily
reflect the views of the publisher, and the publisher
hereby disclaims any responsibility for them.

Any people depicted in stock imagery provided
by Thinkstock are models, and such images are
being used for illustrative purposes only.
Certain stock imagery © Thinkstock.

ISBN: 978-1-4808-3730-0 (sc)
ISBN: 978-1-4808-3731-7 (hc)
ISBN: 978-1-4808-3729-4 (e)

Print information available on the last page.

Archway Publishing rev. date: 10/27/2016

Once upon a time, there was a lion named Dandy who lived in the Northern Arizona Mountains. Dandy the Lion was not only called the "King of Beasts," but he was also called the "King of Kindness." He loved climbing the mountains and looking at everything below him.

One day
while on a tall
mountainside,
Dandy noticed a
raccoon that had fallen
into a deep hole. The
raccoon cried and
cried, not knowing
that Dandy could
see him from up
above.

Dandy raced down from the mountain,
and stopped just above the hole.

As he peered below, the raccoon looked up and was very scared. Finally, the raccoon realized that Dandy was there to help him!

Dandy lowered and stretched his tail until the raccoon could reach it and pull himself up.

Soon he was up on solid ground. He exclaimed, "My name is Ricky. Thank you for saving me from that deep, dark hole! How can I ever repay you?"

Dandy replied, "Just help someone else. That is all I could ever ask!"

Ricky scurried away. Dandy soon made it back up to his favorite shady tree on the side of the mountain, to take his afternoon nap.

On his way home, Ricky came upon a little mouse that had become tangled in some fishing line.

The mouse was scared and pleaded "I can't get out, can you please help me?"

Remembering what Dandy had told him,
Ricky chewed through the fishing line
and soon the mouse was free.

"My name is Milly. Thank you for freeing me from that fishing line! What can I ever do to repay you?"

Ricky replied, "A lion helped me once, and if you help someone else someday, that is all I could ever ask!"

As Milly the Mouse scampered home, she came upon a crying baby Blue Jay. "Why are you crying little one?" asked Milly.

"I fell from my nest, and I can't fly yet," replied the little blue bird.

So Milly put the baby Blue Jay on her back and gave him a ride all the way up the tree, where she gently placed him back into his nest.

Mother Blue Jay was so relieved, and happily chirped, "You saved baby Benny! How can I ever repay you?"

Milly replied, "A raccoon helped me once, and a lion helped him. If you help someone else someday, that is all I could ever ask!"

After Dandy the Lion awoke from his nap, he decided to go for an afternoon dip. Oh, how he loved splashing and swimming with the fish in the pond!

As he climbed out of the water, he stepped on a sharp thorn. "Ouch!" he exclaimed, just as Mother Blue Jay was gliding down to the pond to catch worms.

Remembering what Milly had told her, she knew just what to do! She swooped down, gripped the thorn with her beak, and the next thing Dandy knew, the thorn was out!

"Thank you for pulling that thorn out of my paw! I'm Dandy, what can I do to repay you?"

She replied, "A mouse helped me once, and she said she was helped by a raccoon, who was helped by a lion. If you help someone else someday, that is all I could ever ask!"

That night as Dandy lay in his den, he couldn't help but smile with delight. He thought about how good it felt to help his friends, and to have their help too!

The End

Sharing time!

Dandy the Lion was not only the "King of Beasts," but he was also known as the "King of Kindness!" He mentioned at the end of the story about how good it felt to help his friends. Here are a few questions that will give you the opportunity for open communication and dialog:

1. Why do you think it is important to help others?

2. Name a time when someone helped you.

3. How did it feel when someone helped you?

4. Name a time when you helped someone?

5. How did it feel to help someone?

6. Name three ways you can help others.

_____

_____

_____

CPSIA information can be obtained
at www.ICGtesting.com
Printed in the USA
LVOW06*0809191216

517916LV00018B/330/P